City Birds

A nearly true story about peregrine falcons who nested on a city building

By

Dean Norman

STAR BRIGHT BOOKS
CAMBRIDGE, MASSACHUSETTS

Published by Star Bright Books in 2015

Copyright © 2015 Dean Norman

All rights reserved. No part of this book may be reproduced or transmitted in any form or by any means that are available now or in the future, without permission in writing from the copyright holder and the publisher.

The name Star Bright Books and the Star Bright Books logo are registered trademarks of Star Bright Books, Inc. Please visit: www.starbrightbooks.com. For bulk orders, please email: orders@starbrightbooks.com, or call customer service at: (617) 354-1300.

Printed on paper from sustainable forests

ISBN-13: 978-1-59572-708-4
Star Bright Books / MA / 00109150
Printed in China / JADE / 0 9 8 7 6 5 4 3 2 1

Library of Congress Cataloging-in-Publication Data

Norman, Dean, author, illustrator.
 City birds : a nearly true story about peregrine falcons who nested on a city building / by Dean Norman.
      pages cm
 Summary: "Atop a skyscraper in Cleveland, Ohio, two falcon hatchlings, with their parents' guidance, learn to catch pigeons, how to interact with humans, and how to fly, the final skill that will alllow them to leave their concrete home and hunt for food and start their own homes and family"-- Provided by publisher.
 Includes bibliographical references.
ISBN 978-1-59572-708-4 (pbk. : alk. paper)
1. Graphic novels. [1. Graphic novels. 2. Peregrine falcon--Fiction. 3. Falcons--Fiction.] I. Title.
PZ7.7.N675Ci 2015
741.5'973--dc23
                              2015026482

Dedicated to Sara Jean Peters

A wildlife officer who told the story of the city birds to many audiences, and enjoyed the times when my cartoon version of the story was included.

Once upon a time not so long ago, two peregrine falcons decided to nest on a window ledge of a tall building in downtown Cleveland, Ohio. People helped them by putting a box of gravel on the ledge so the eggs wouldn't roll off before the chicks hatched. On the 4th of July holiday, there was going to be a problem. Fireworks would be shot from the top of the building, and the Cleveland Orchestra would play in a park next to the building. Would the falcons be scared away and their eggs never hatch?

Well, the fireworks were shot from another building, but the concert had to go on because so many people wanted to enjoy it. The falcons calmly watched the 4th of July show and didn't leave their nest. The last tune played by the orchestra was "Stars and Stripes Forever", and that is why the two falcon chicks were named "Stars" and "Stripes". A TV camera was set up to show the falcon nest so everyone in Cleveland could see the chicks hatch and grow up. That show began the day after the fireworks and concert.

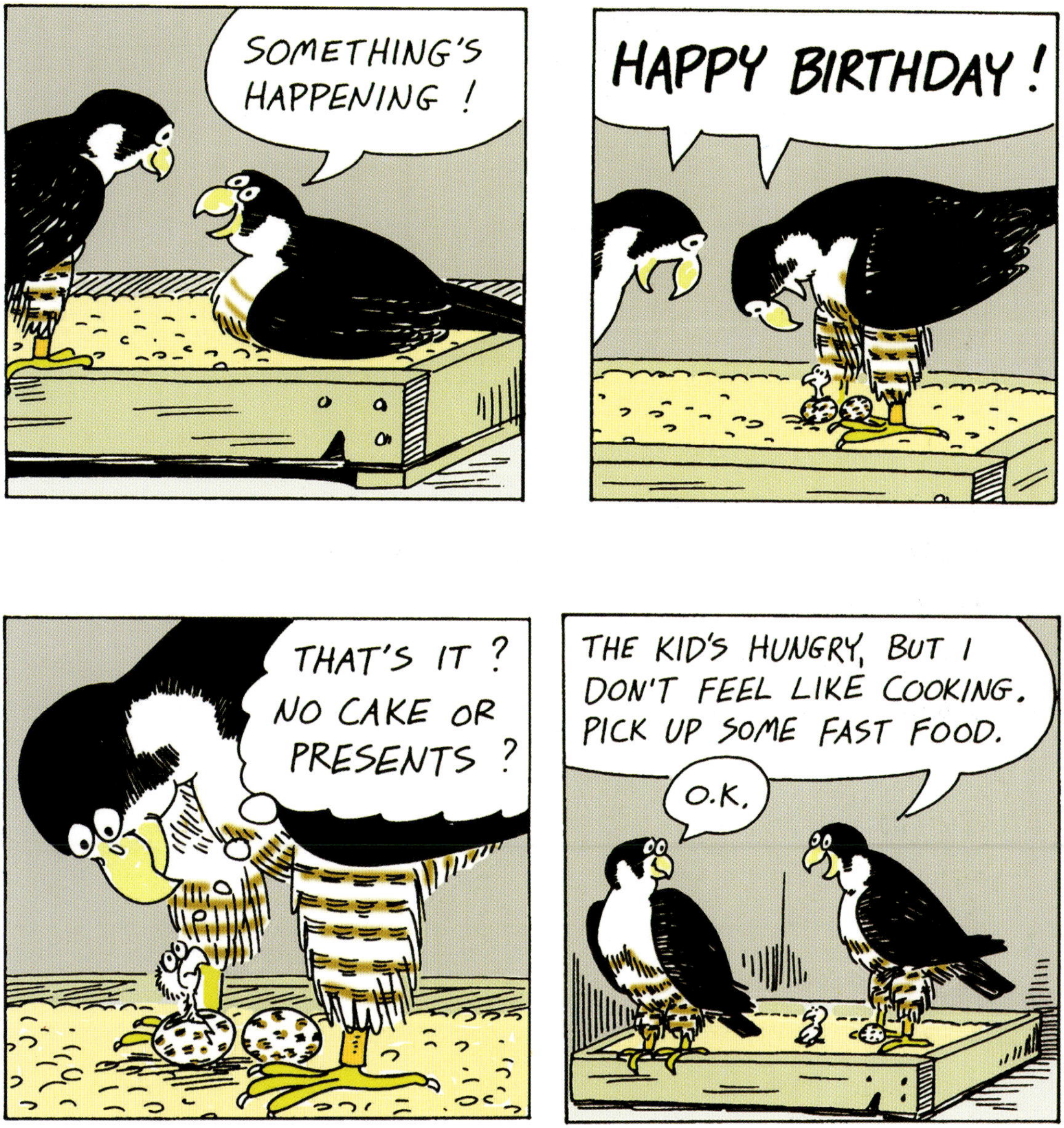
SOMETHING'S HAPPENING !
HAPPY BIRTHDAY !
THAT'S IT ? NO CAKE OR PRESENTS ?
THE KID'S HUNGRY, BUT I DON'T FEEL LIKE COOKING. PICK UP SOME FAST FOOD.
O.K.

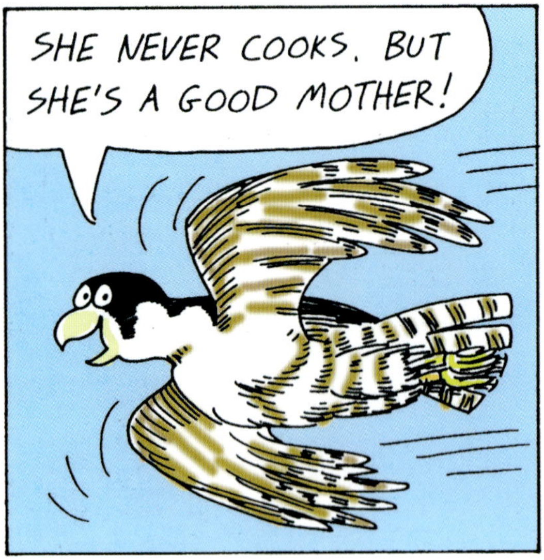
SHE NEVER COOKS. BUT SHE'S A GOOD MOTHER!

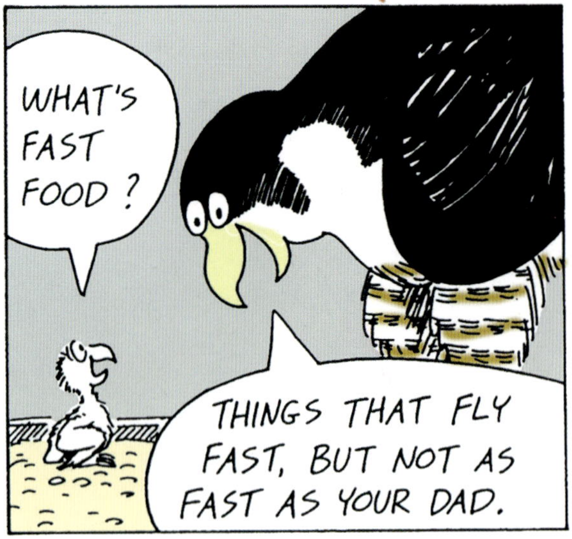
WHAT'S FAST FOOD ?
THINGS THAT FLY FAST, BUT NOT AS FAST AS YOUR DAD.

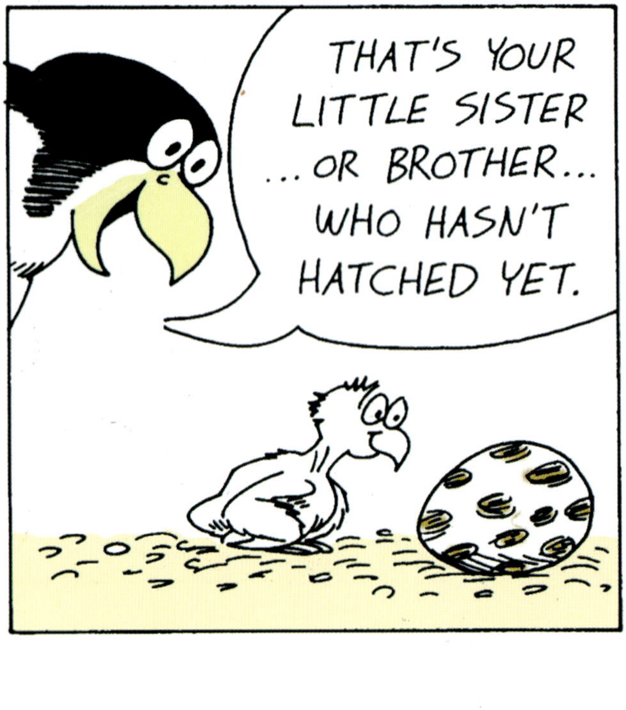
THAT'S YOUR LITTLE SISTER ...OR BROTHER... WHO HASN'T HATCHED YET.

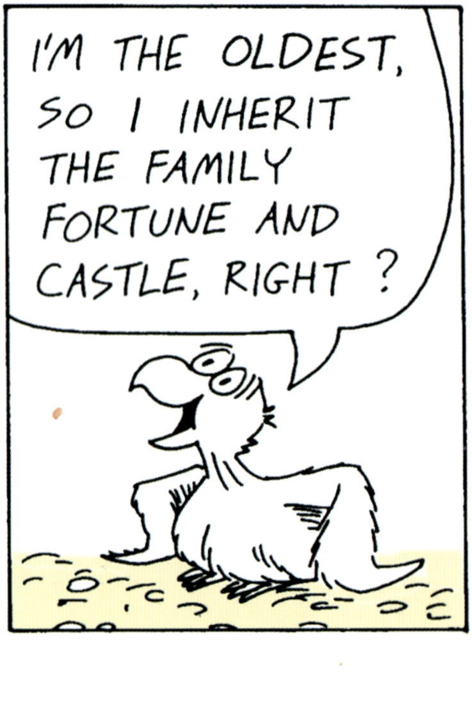
I'M THE OLDEST, SO I INHERIT THE FAMILY FORTUNE AND CASTLE, RIGHT ?

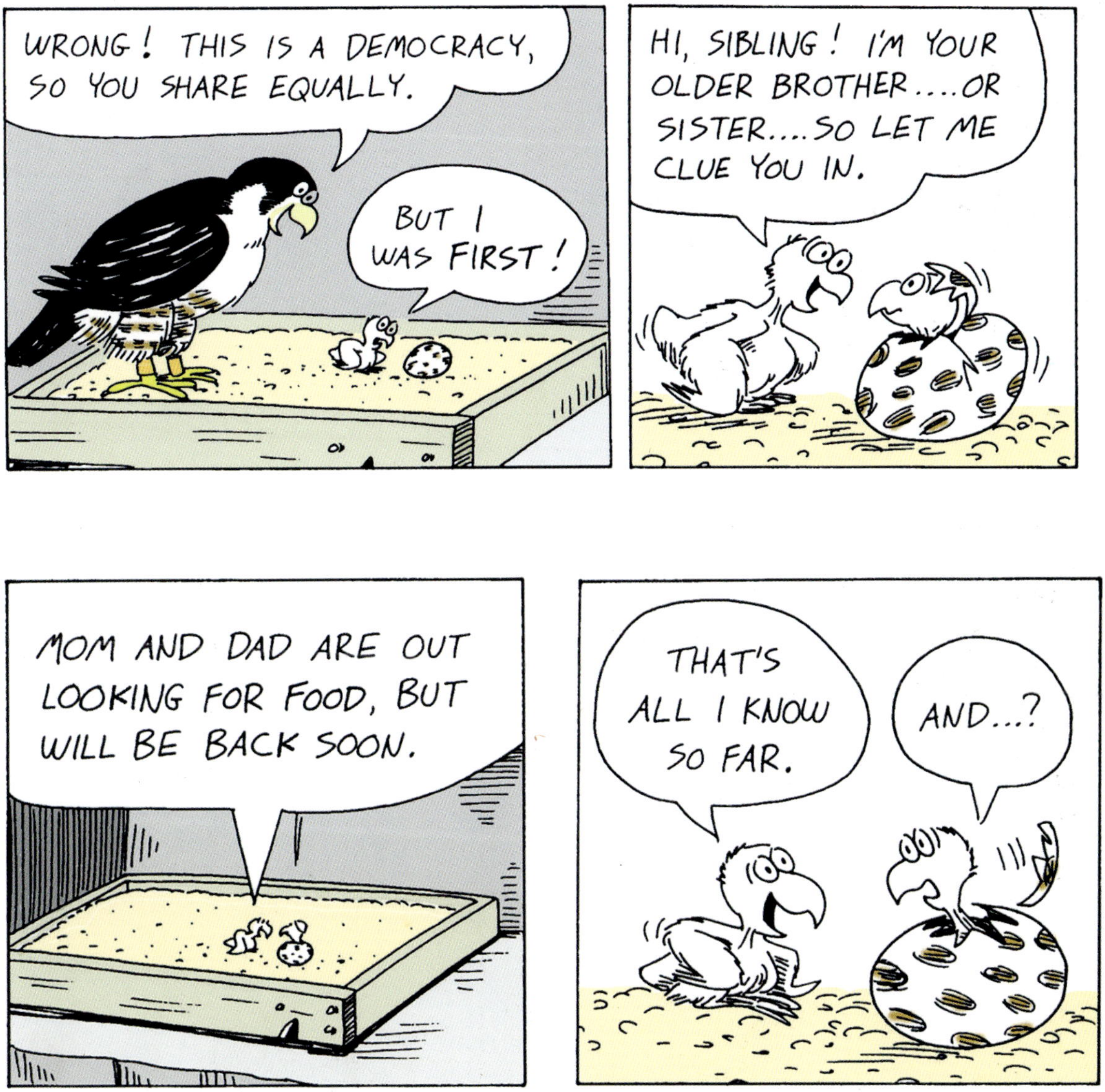
WRONG! THIS IS A DEMOCRACY, SO YOU SHARE EQUALLY.
BUT I WAS FIRST!
HI, SIBLING! I'M YOUR OLDER BROTHER....OR SISTER....SO LET ME CLUE YOU IN.
MOM AND DAD ARE OUT LOOKING FOR FOOD, BUT WILL BE BACK SOON.
THAT'S ALL I KNOW SO FAR.
AND...?

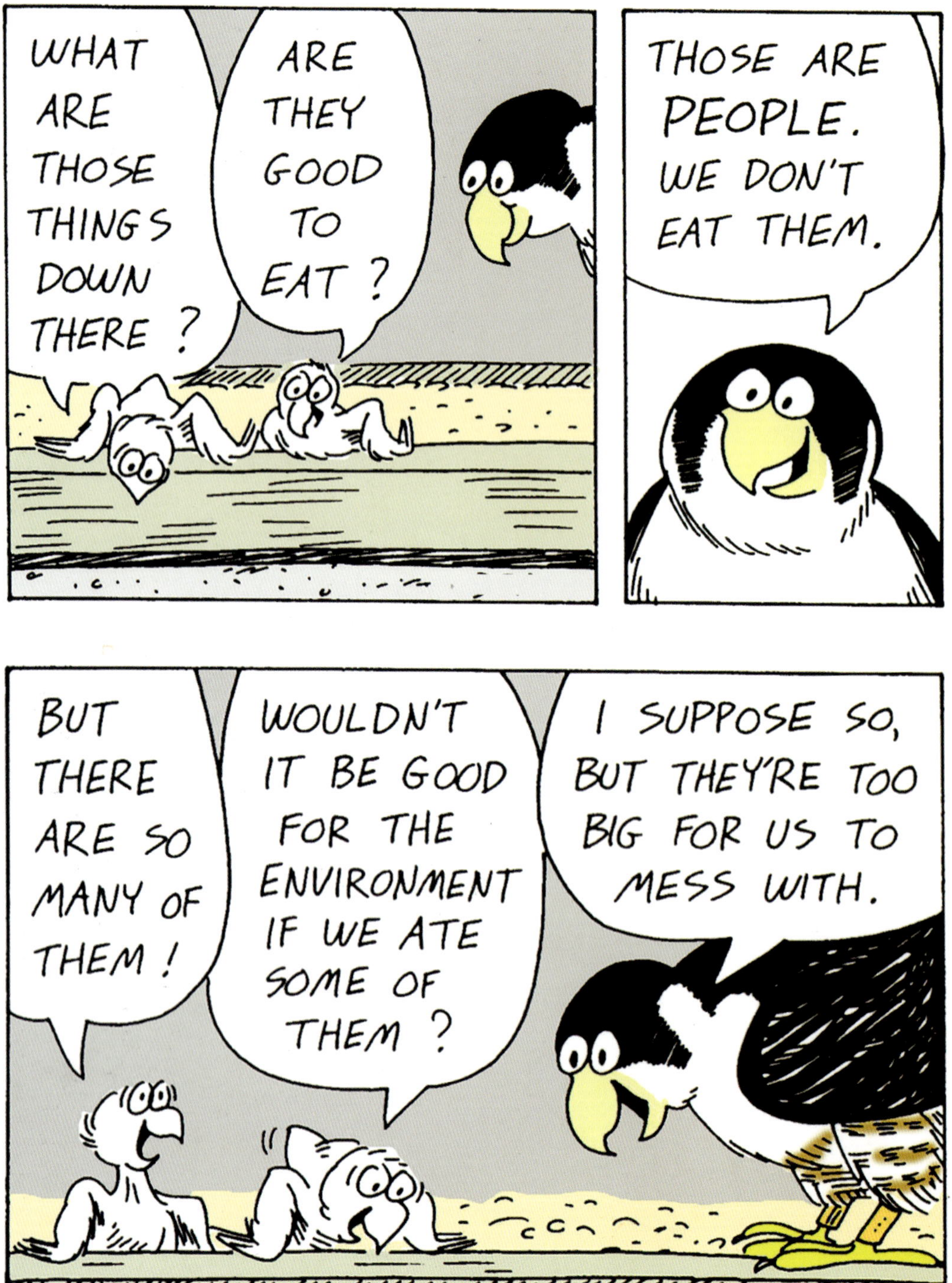
WHAT ARE THOSE THINGS DOWN THERE?
ARE THEY GOOD TO EAT?
THOSE ARE PEOPLE. WE DON'T EAT THEM.
BUT THERE ARE SO MANY OF THEM!
WOULDN'T IT BE GOOD FOR THE ENVIRONMENT IF WE ATE SOME OF THEM?
I SUPPOSE SO, BUT THEY'RE TOO BIG FOR US TO MESS WITH.

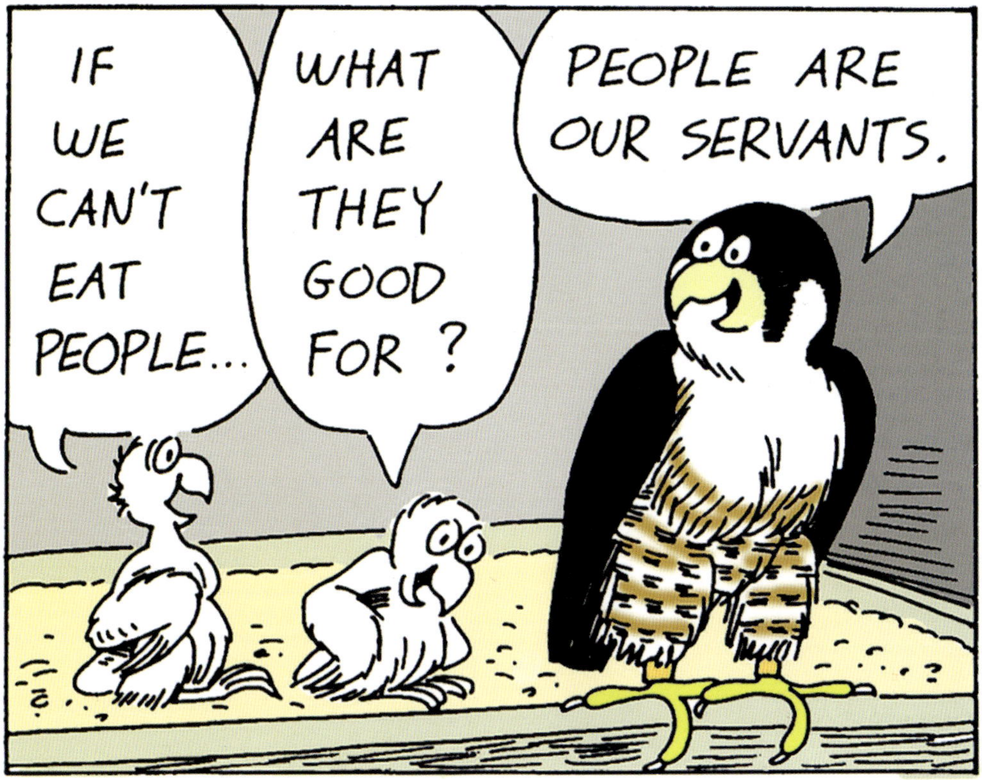
IF WE CAN'T EAT PEOPLE...
WHAT ARE THEY GOOD FOR ?
PEOPLE ARE OUR SERVANTS.

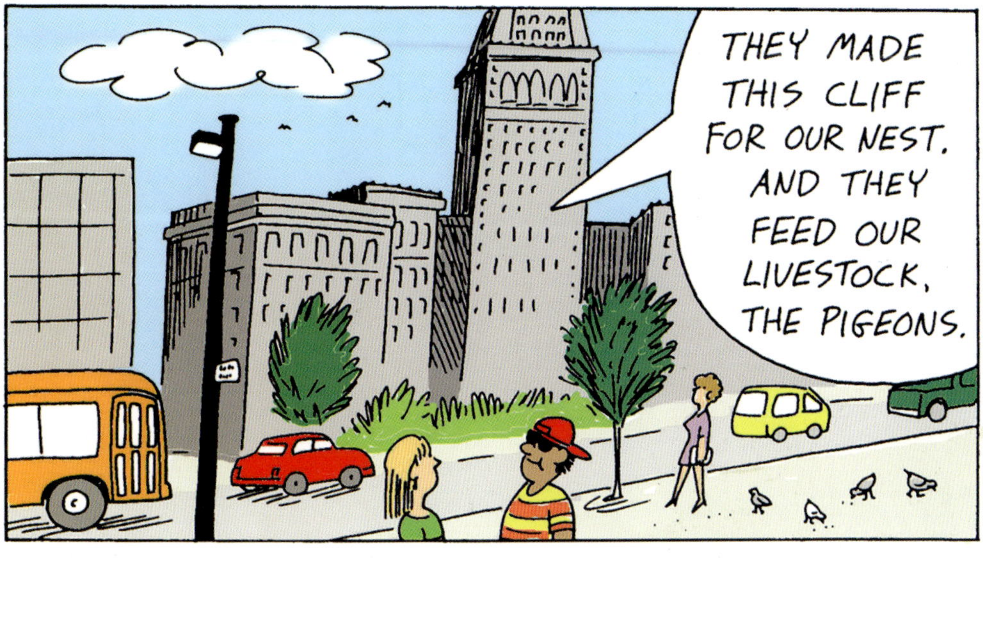
THEY MADE THIS CLIFF FOR OUR NEST. AND THEY FEED OUR LIVESTOCK, THE PIGEONS.

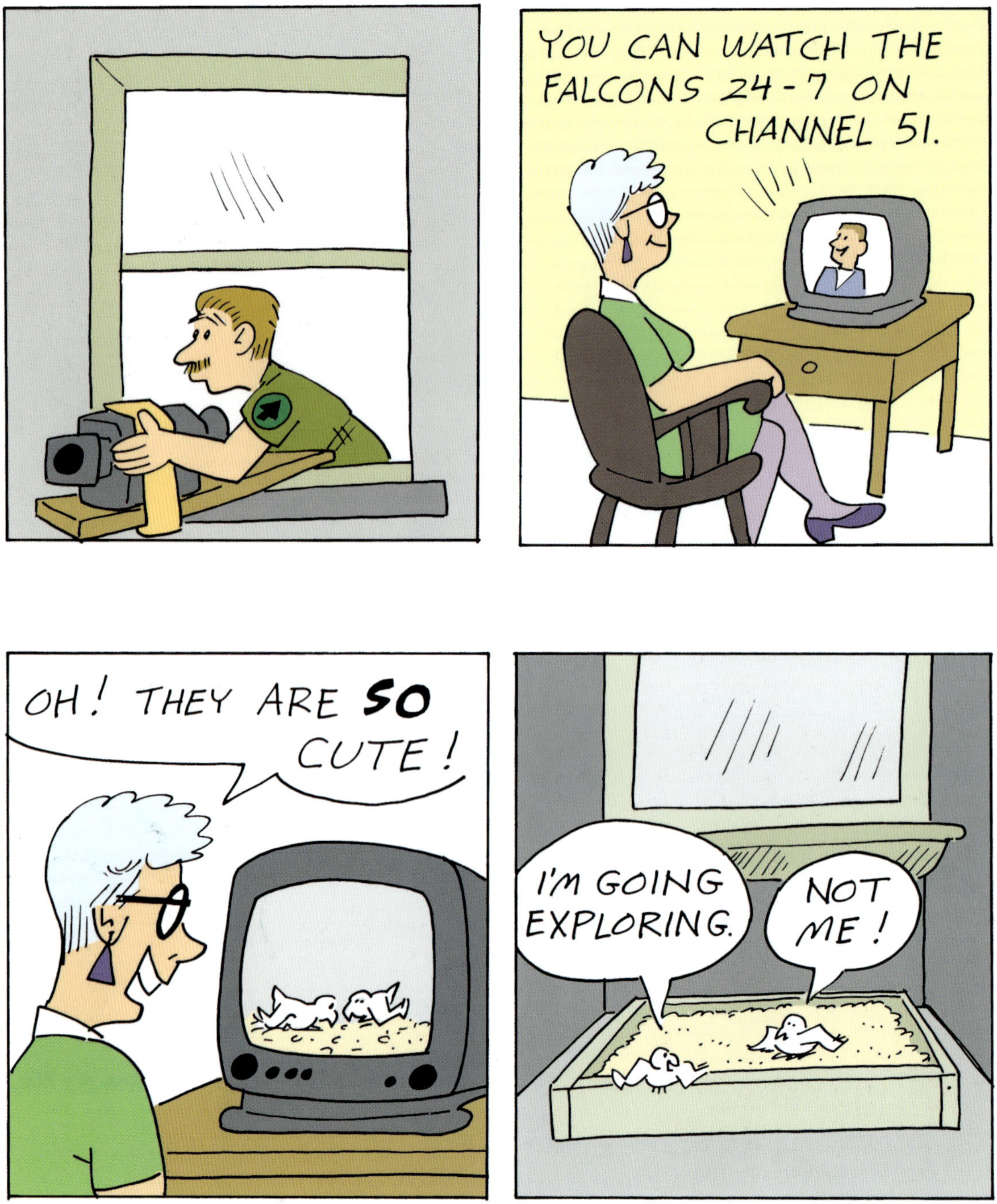
YOU CAN WATCH THE FALCONS 24-7 ON CHANNEL 51.
OH! THEY ARE **SO** CUTE!
I'M GOING EXPLORING.
NOT ME!

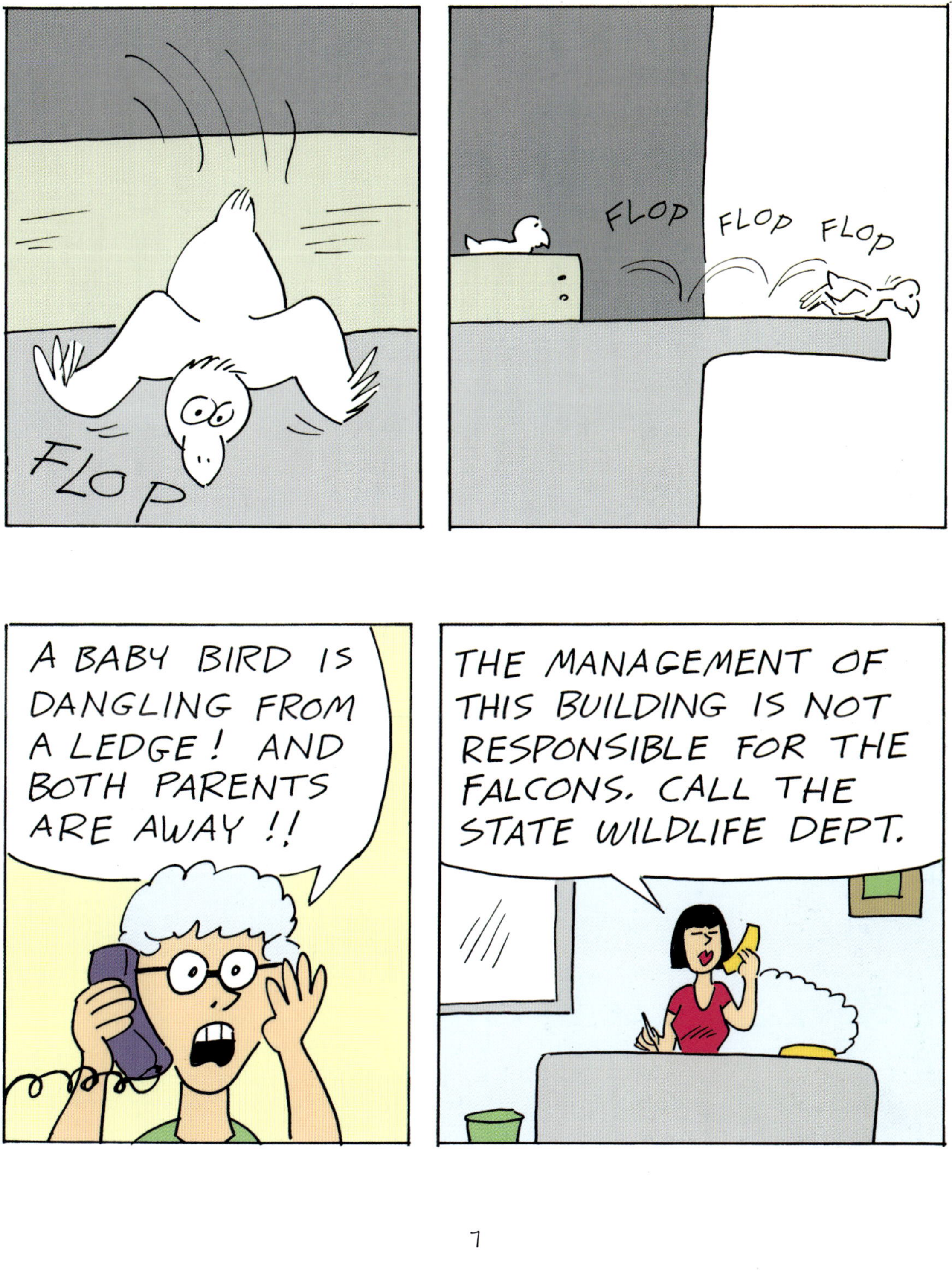
FLOP
FLOP
FLOP
FLOP
A BABY BIRD IS DANGLING FROM A LEDGE! AND BOTH PARENTS ARE AWAY!!
THE MANAGEMENT OF THIS BUILDING IS NOT RESPONSIBLE FOR THE FALCONS. CALL THE STATE WILDLIFE DEPT.

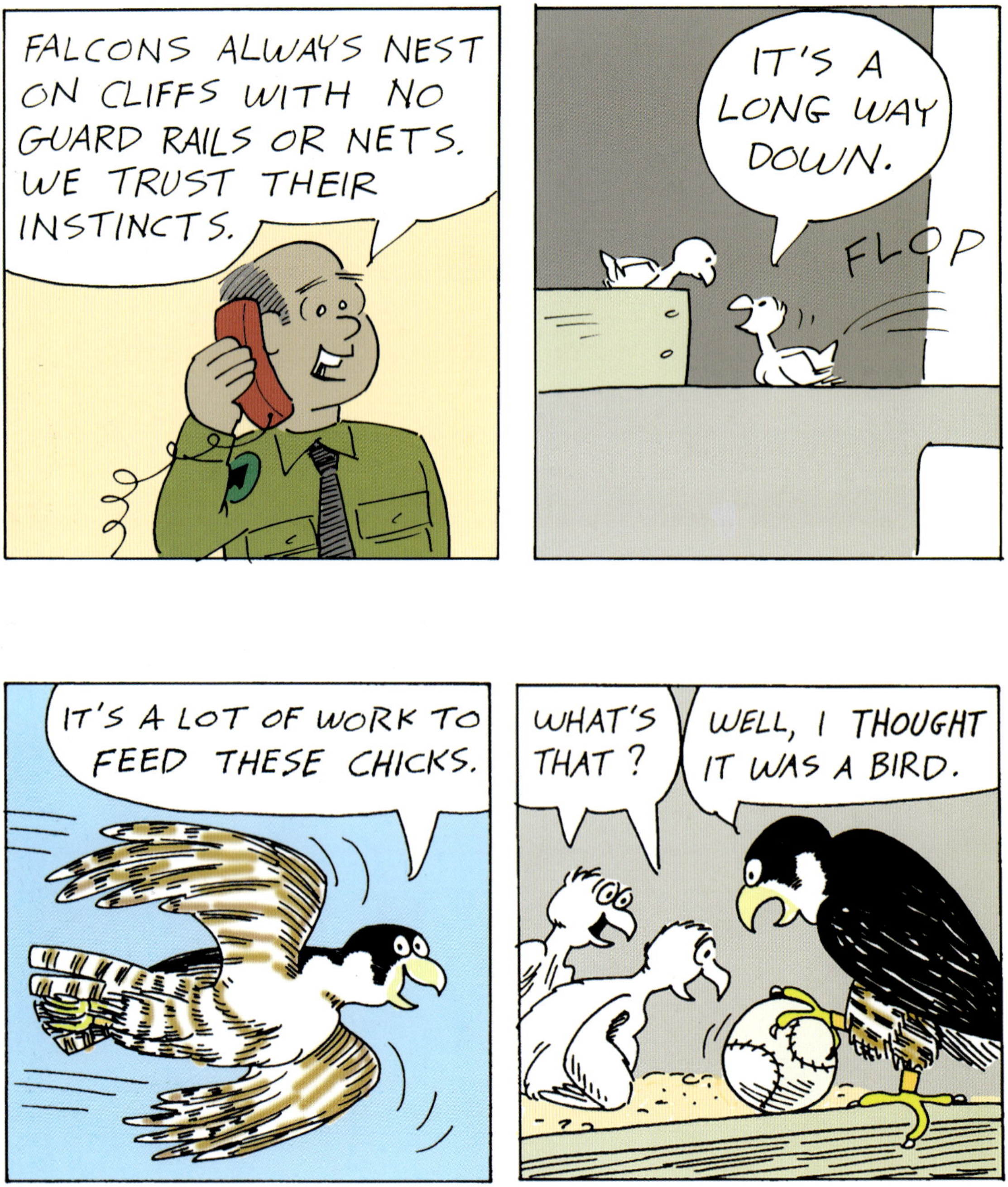
FALCONS ALWAYS NEST ON CLIFFS WITH NO GUARD RAILS OR NETS. WE TRUST THEIR INSTINCTS.
IT'S A LONG WAY DOWN.
FLOP
IT'S A LOT OF WORK TO FEED THESE CHICKS.
WHAT'S THAT?
WELL, I THOUGHT IT WAS A BIRD.

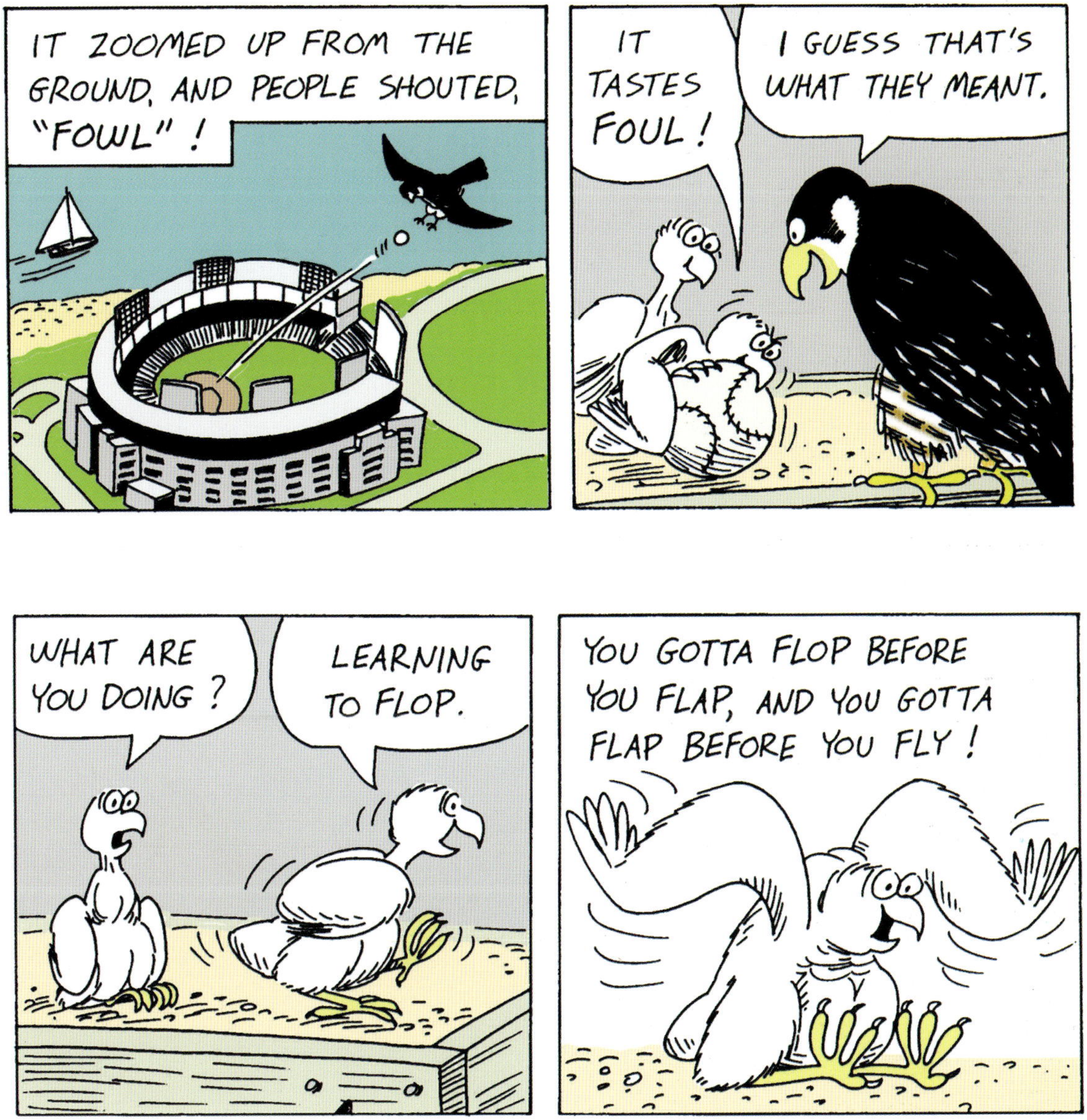
IT ZOOMED UP FROM THE GROUND, AND PEOPLE SHOUTED, "FOWL"!
IT TASTES FOUL!
I GUESS THAT'S WHAT THEY MEANT.
WHAT ARE YOU DOING?
LEARNING TO FLOP.
YOU GOTTA FLOP BEFORE YOU FLAP, AND YOU GOTTA FLAP BEFORE YOU FLY!

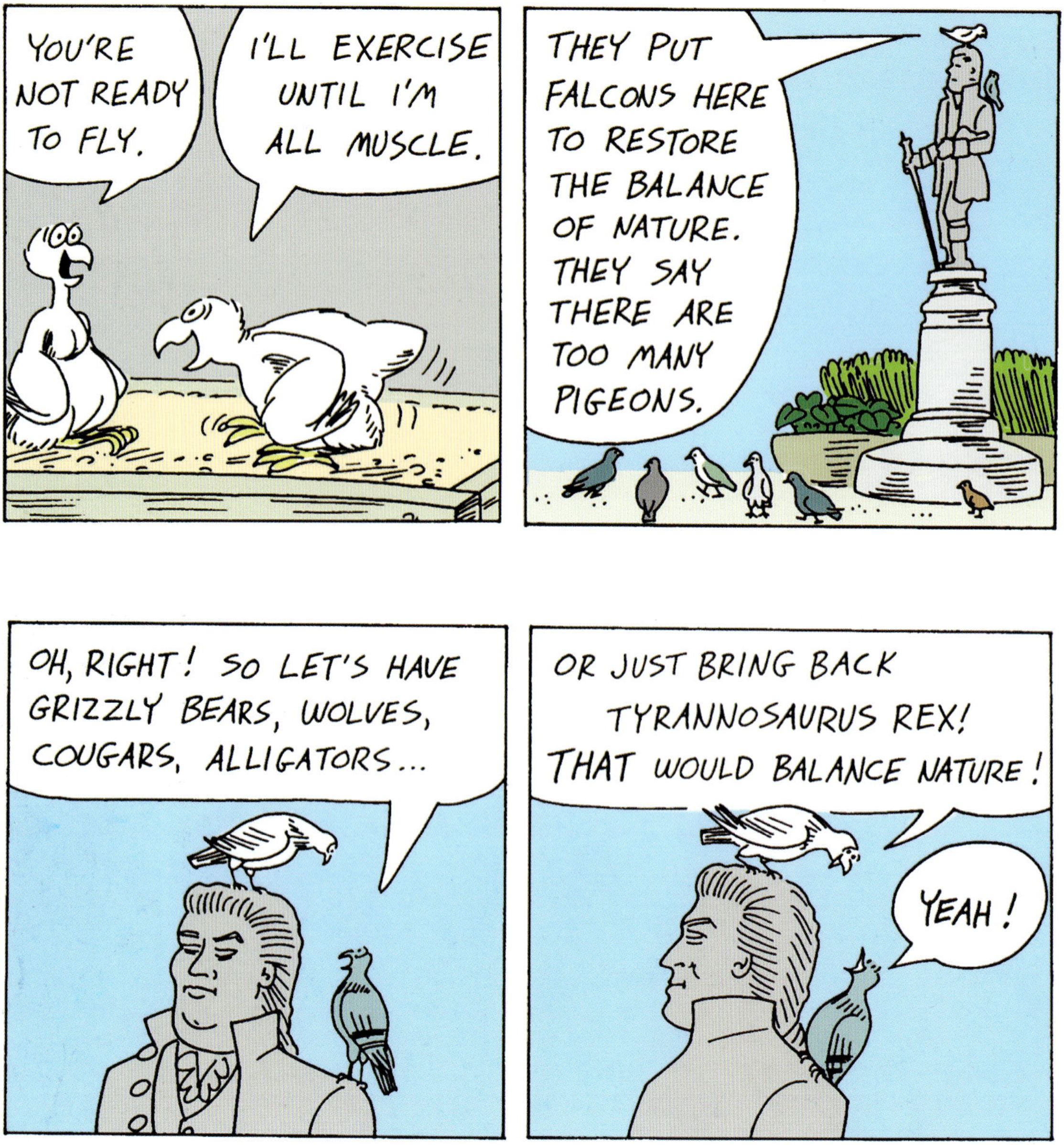
YOU'RE NOT READY TO FLY.
I'LL EXERCISE UNTIL I'M ALL MUSCLE.
THEY PUT FALCONS HERE TO RESTORE THE BALANCE OF NATURE. THEY SAY THERE ARE TOO MANY PIGEONS.
OH, RIGHT! SO LET'S HAVE GRIZZLY BEARS, WOLVES, COUGARS, ALLIGATORS...
OR JUST BRING BACK TYRANNOSAURUS REX! THAT WOULD BALANCE NATURE!
YEAH!

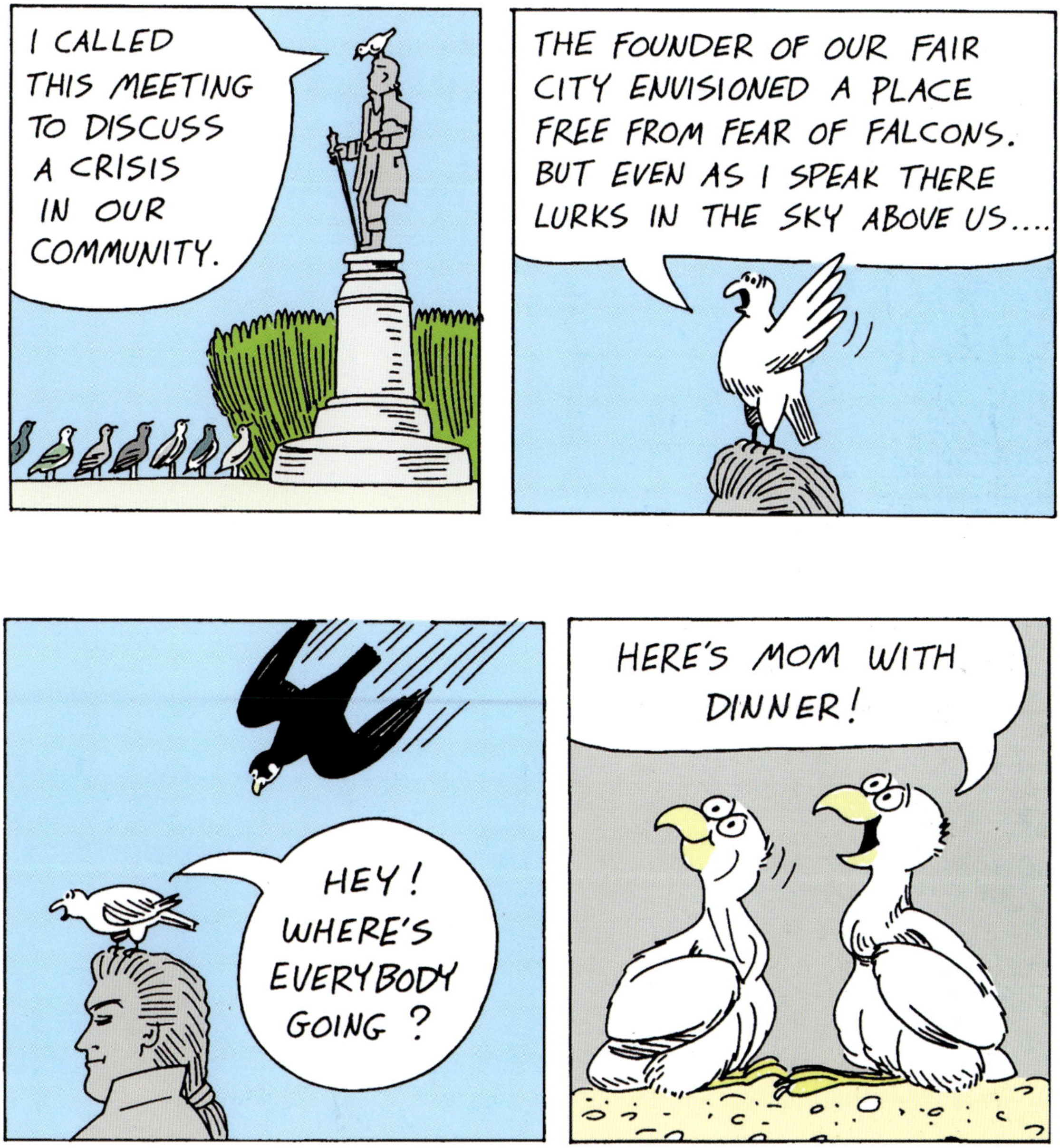
I CALLED THIS MEETING TO DISCUSS A CRISIS IN OUR COMMUNITY.
THE FOUNDER OF OUR FAIR CITY ENVISIONED A PLACE FREE FROM FEAR OF FALCONS. BUT EVEN AS I SPEAK THERE LURKS IN THE SKY ABOVE US....
HEY! WHERE'S EVERYBODY GOING?
HERE'S MOM WITH DINNER!

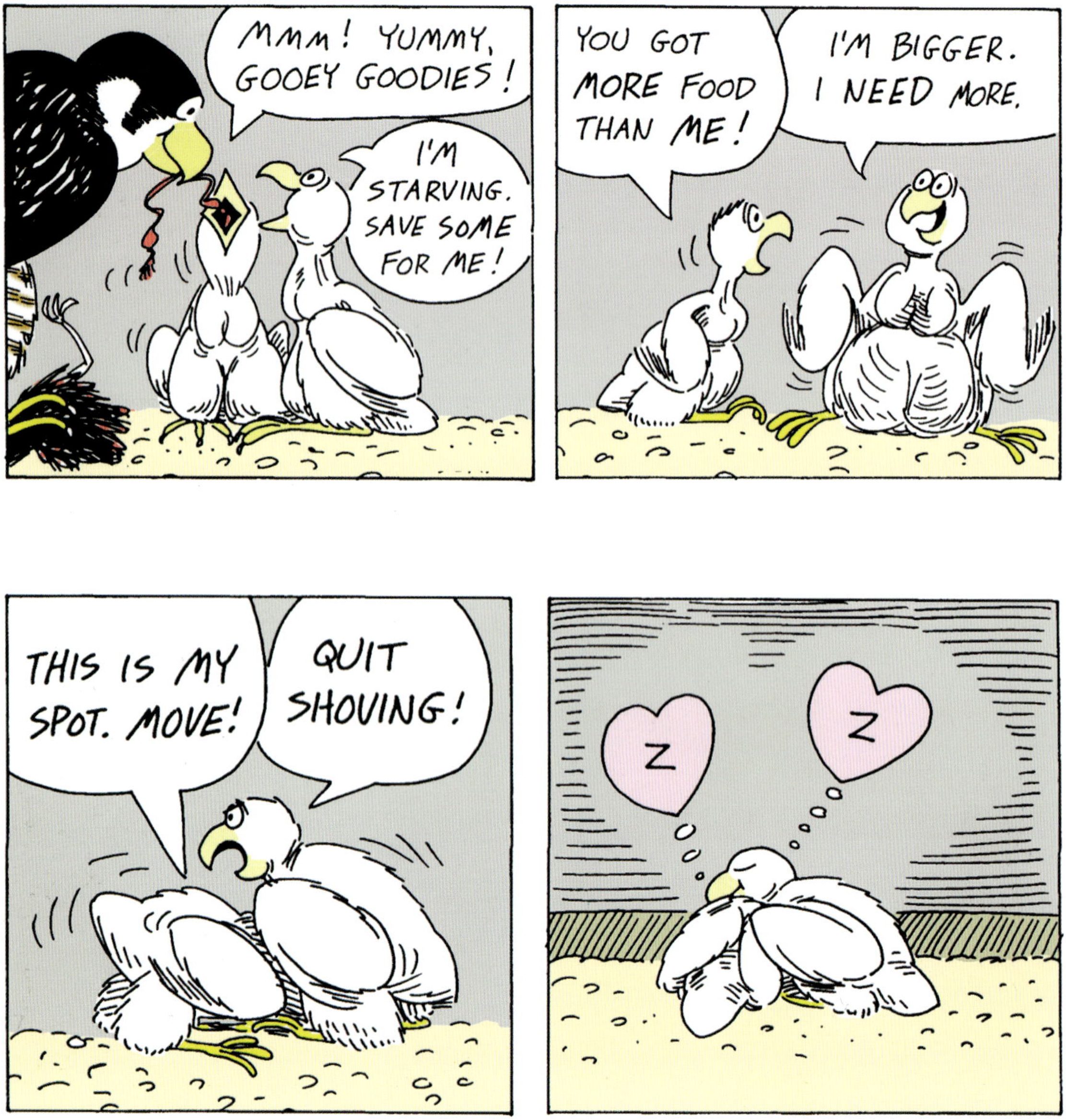
MMM! YUMMY, GOOEY GOODIES!
I'M STARVING. SAVE SOME FOR ME!
YOU GOT MORE FOOD THAN ME!
I'M BIGGER. I NEED MORE.
THIS IS MY SPOT. MOVE!
QUIT SHOVING!
Z
Z

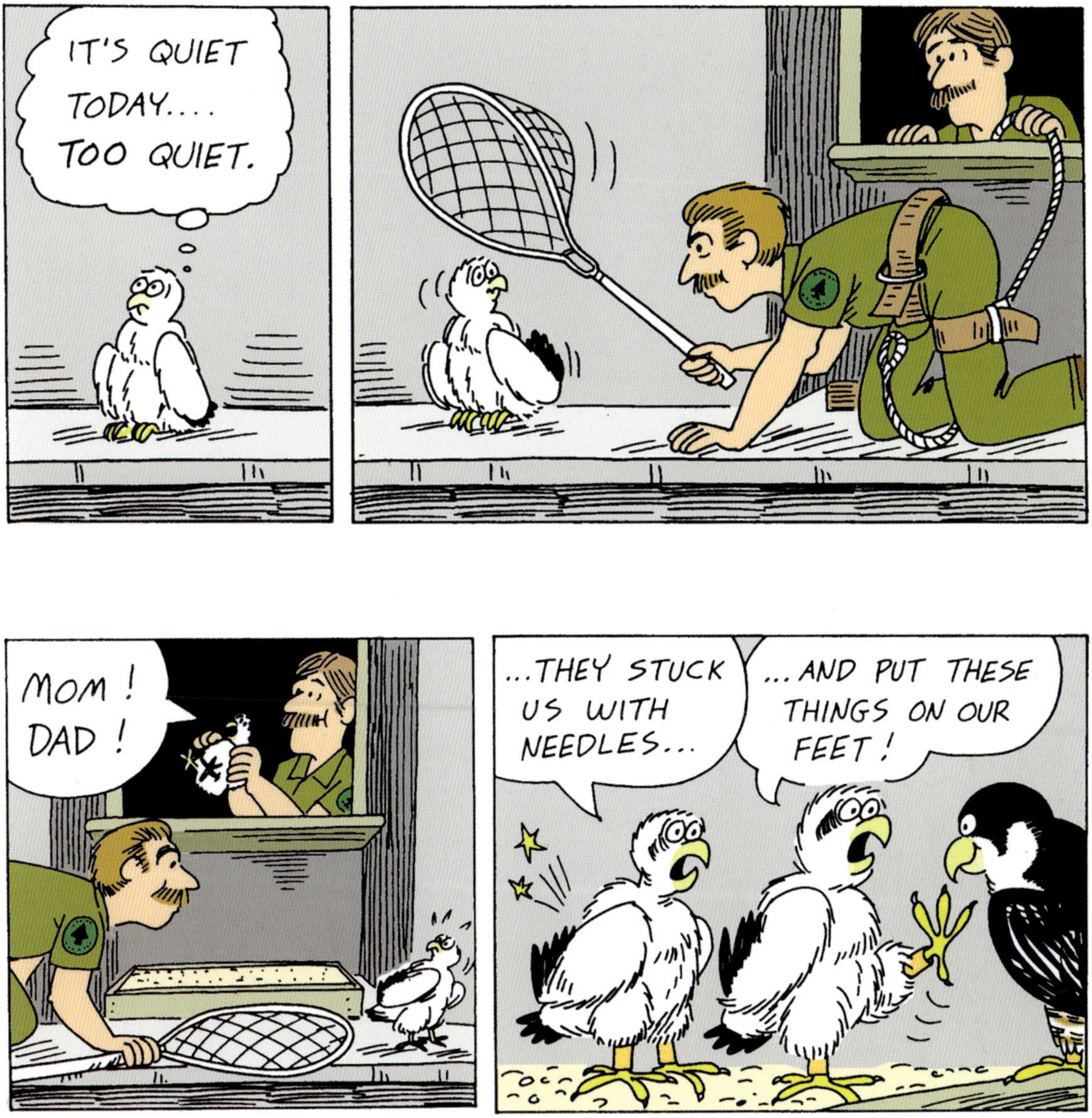
IT'S QUIET TODAY.... TOO QUIET.
MOM ! DAD !
...THEY STUCK US WITH NEEDLES...
...AND PUT THESE THINGS ON OUR FEET !

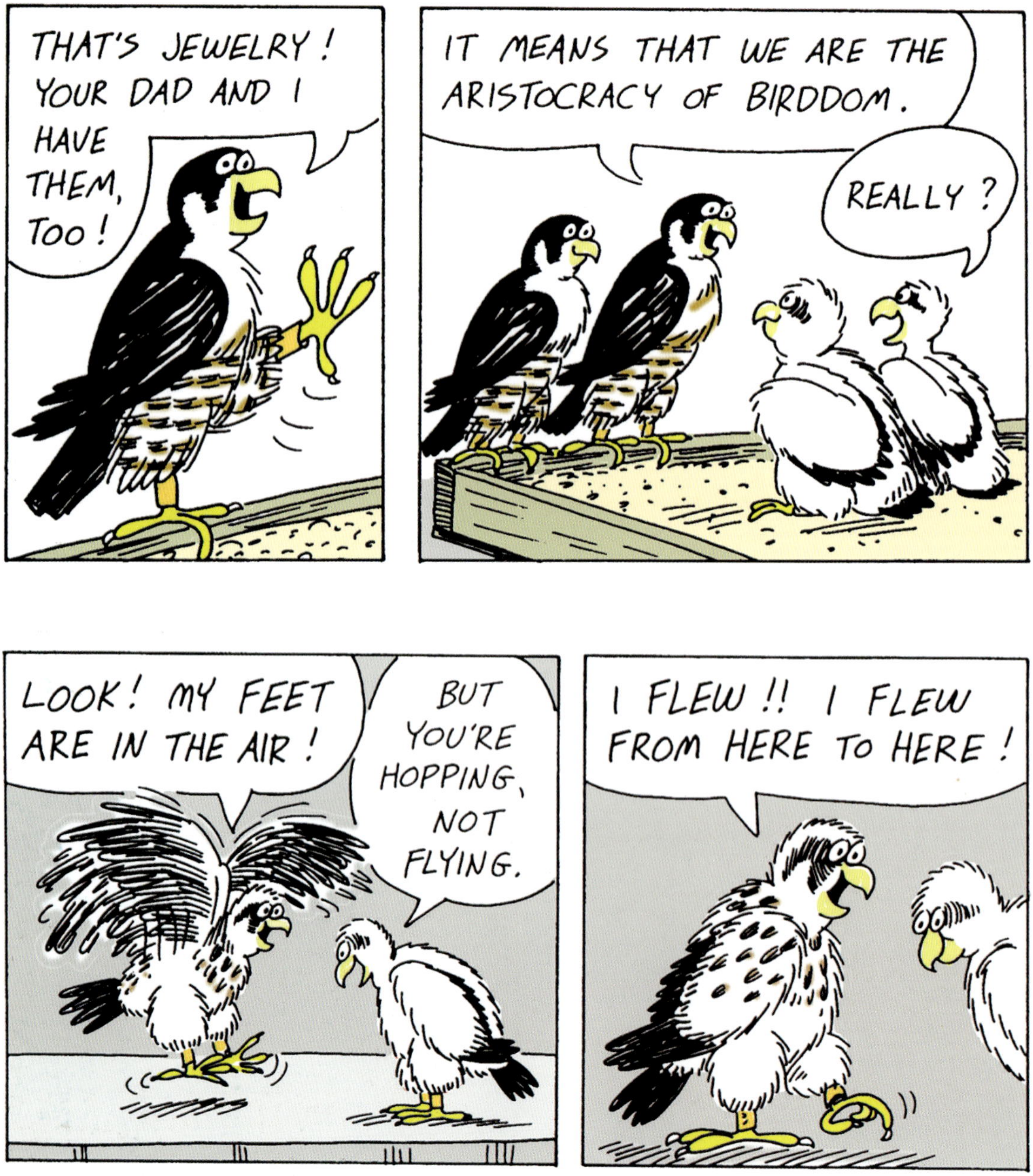
THAT'S JEWELRY! YOUR DAD AND I HAVE THEM, TOO!
IT MEANS THAT WE ARE THE ARISTOCRACY OF BIRDDOM.
REALLY?
LOOK! MY FEET ARE IN THE AIR!
BUT YOU'RE HOPPING, NOT FLYING.
I FLEW!! I FLEW FROM HERE TO HERE!

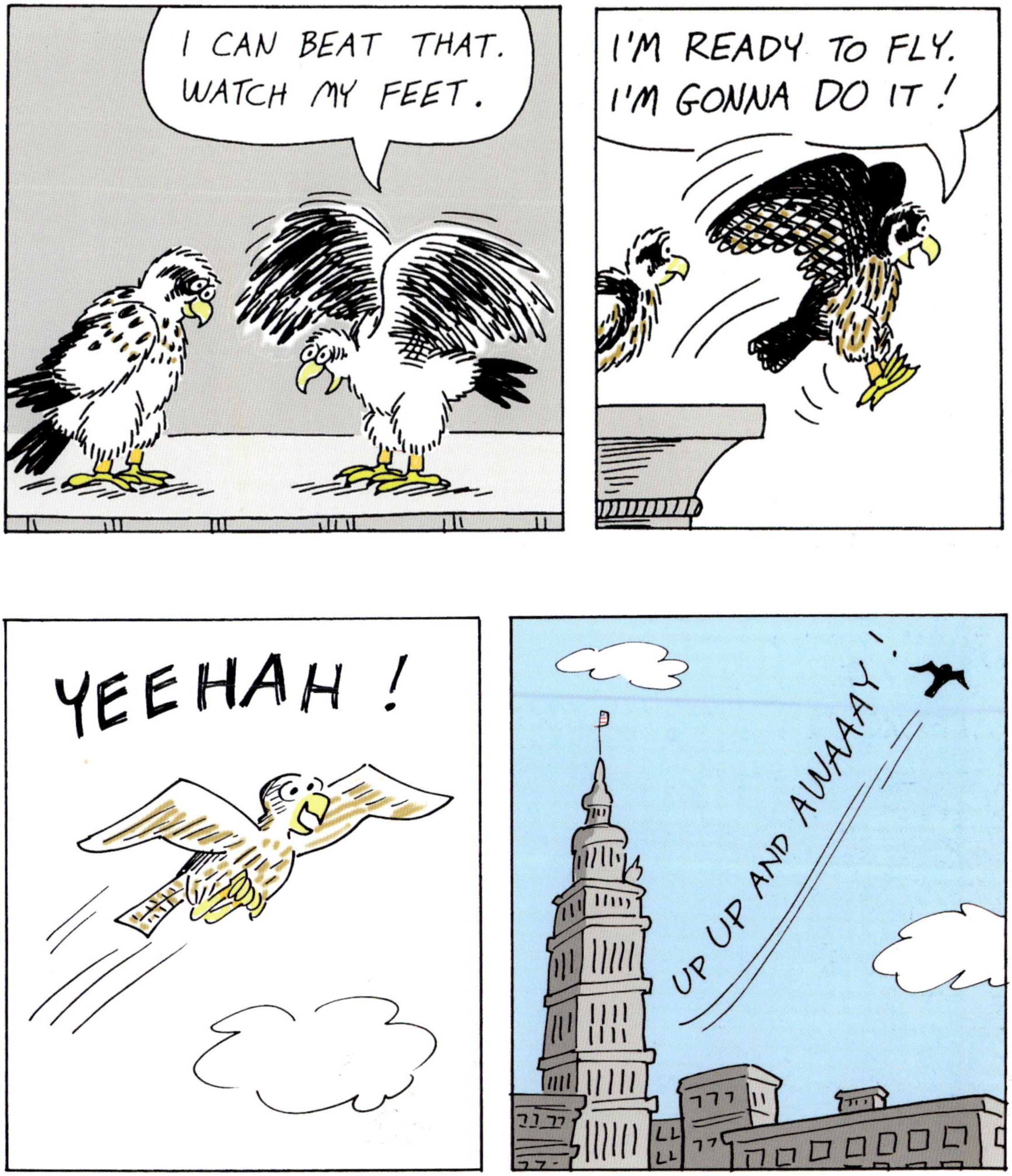
I CAN BEAT THAT. WATCH MY FEET.
I'M READY TO FLY. I'M GONNA DO IT!
YEEHAH!
UP UP AND AWAAAY!

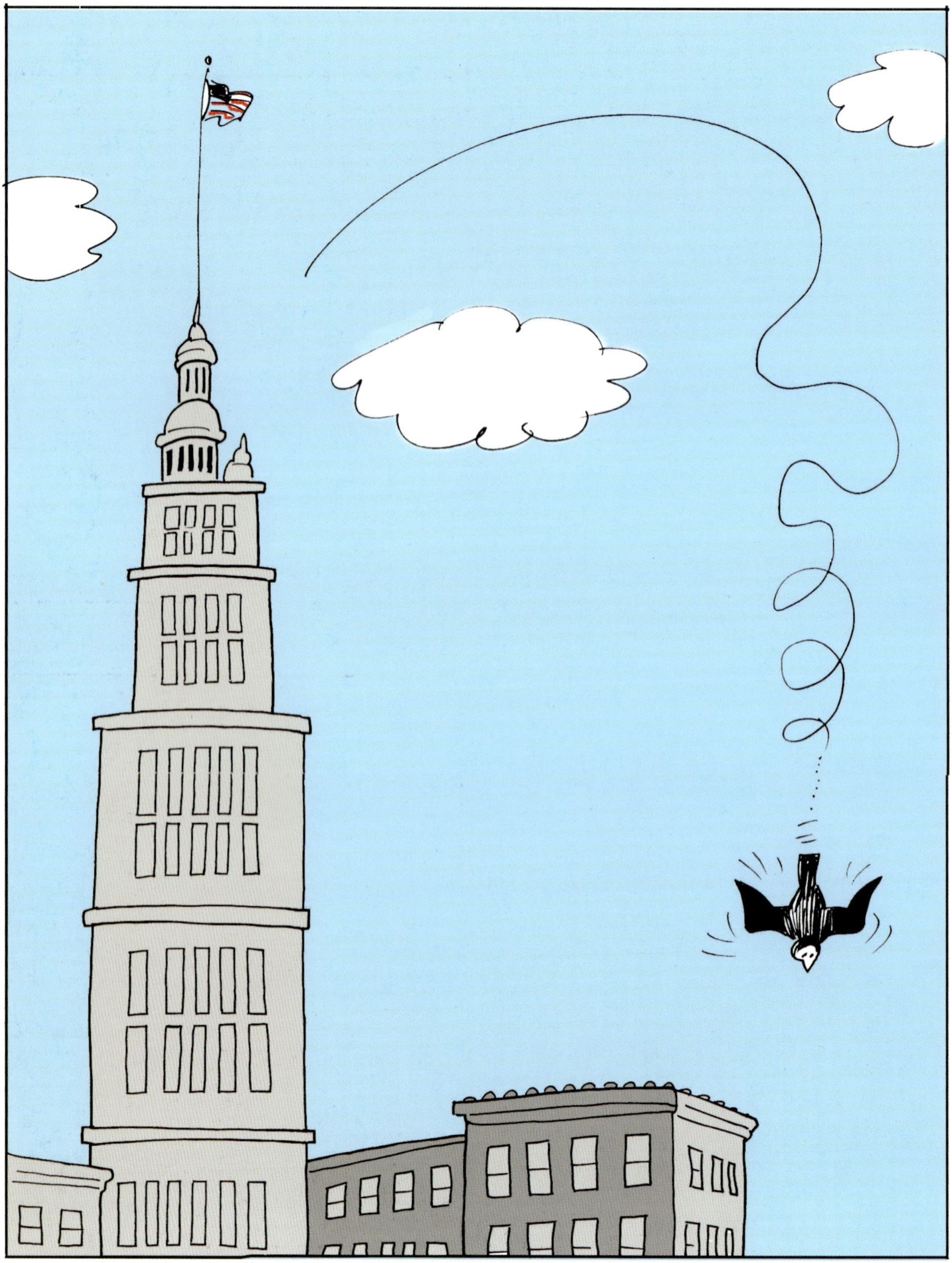

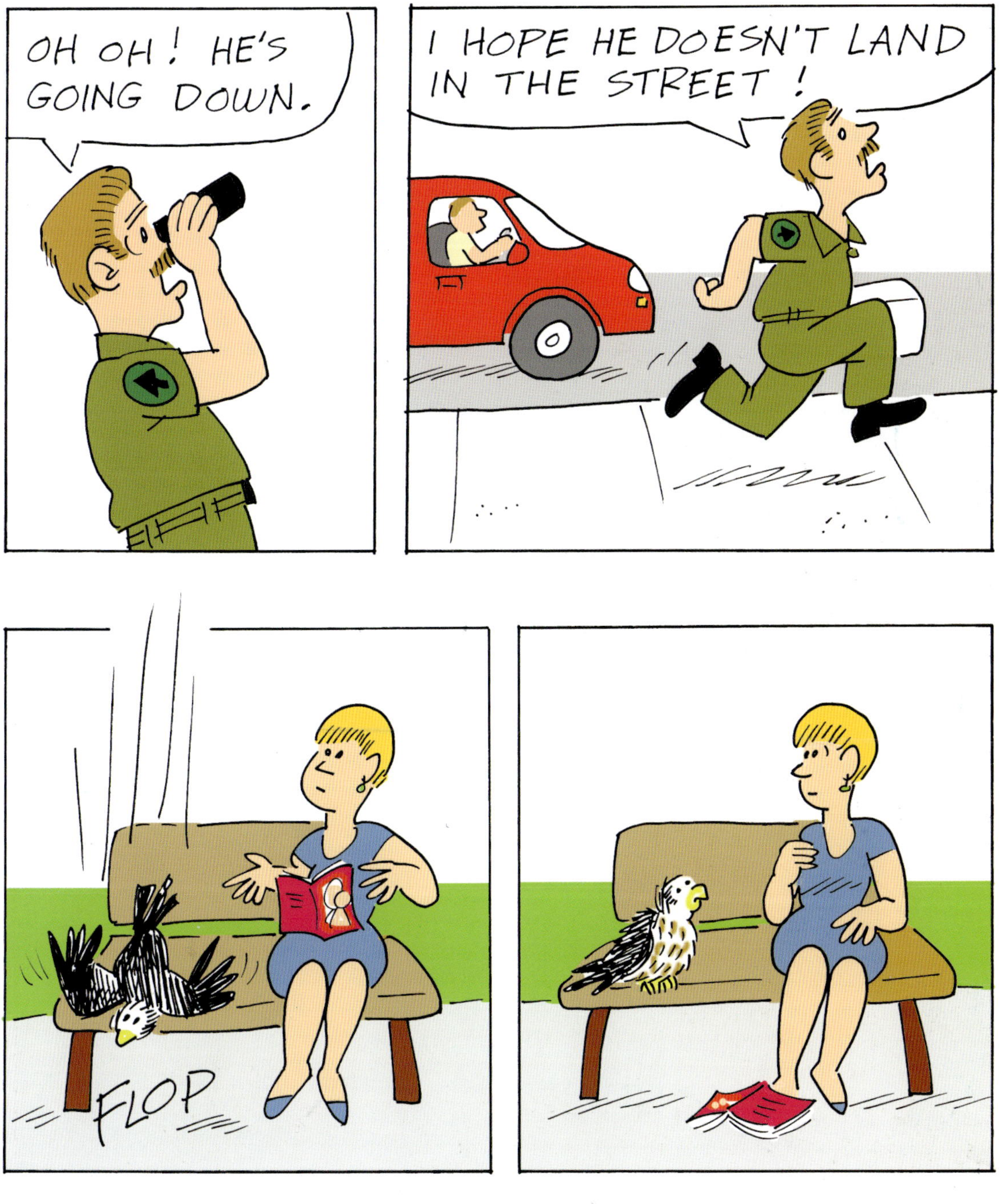
OH OH! HE'S GOING DOWN.
I HOPE HE DOESN'T LAND IN THE STREET!
FLOP

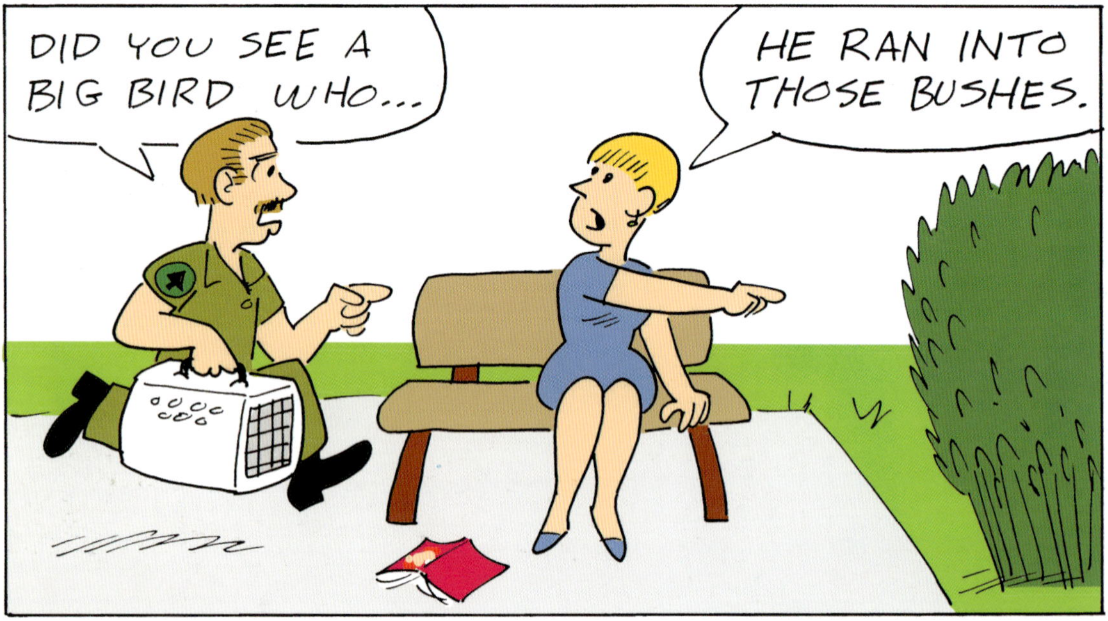
DID YOU SEE A BIG BIRD WHO...
HE RAN INTO THOSE BUSHES.

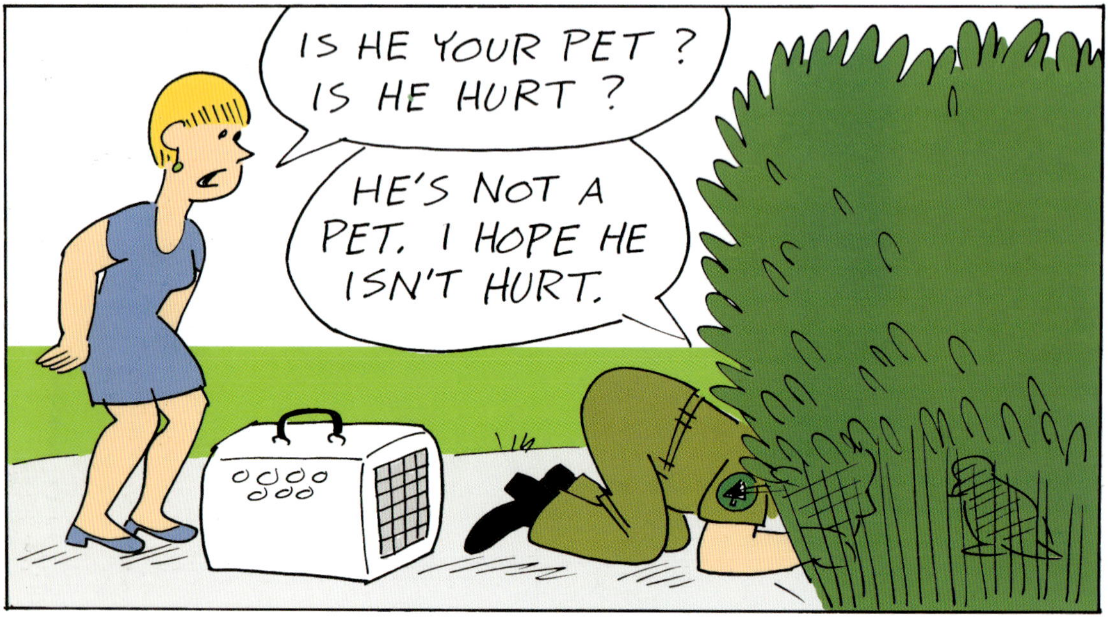
IS HE YOUR PET ? IS HE HURT ?
HE'S NOT A PET. I HOPE HE ISN'T HURT.

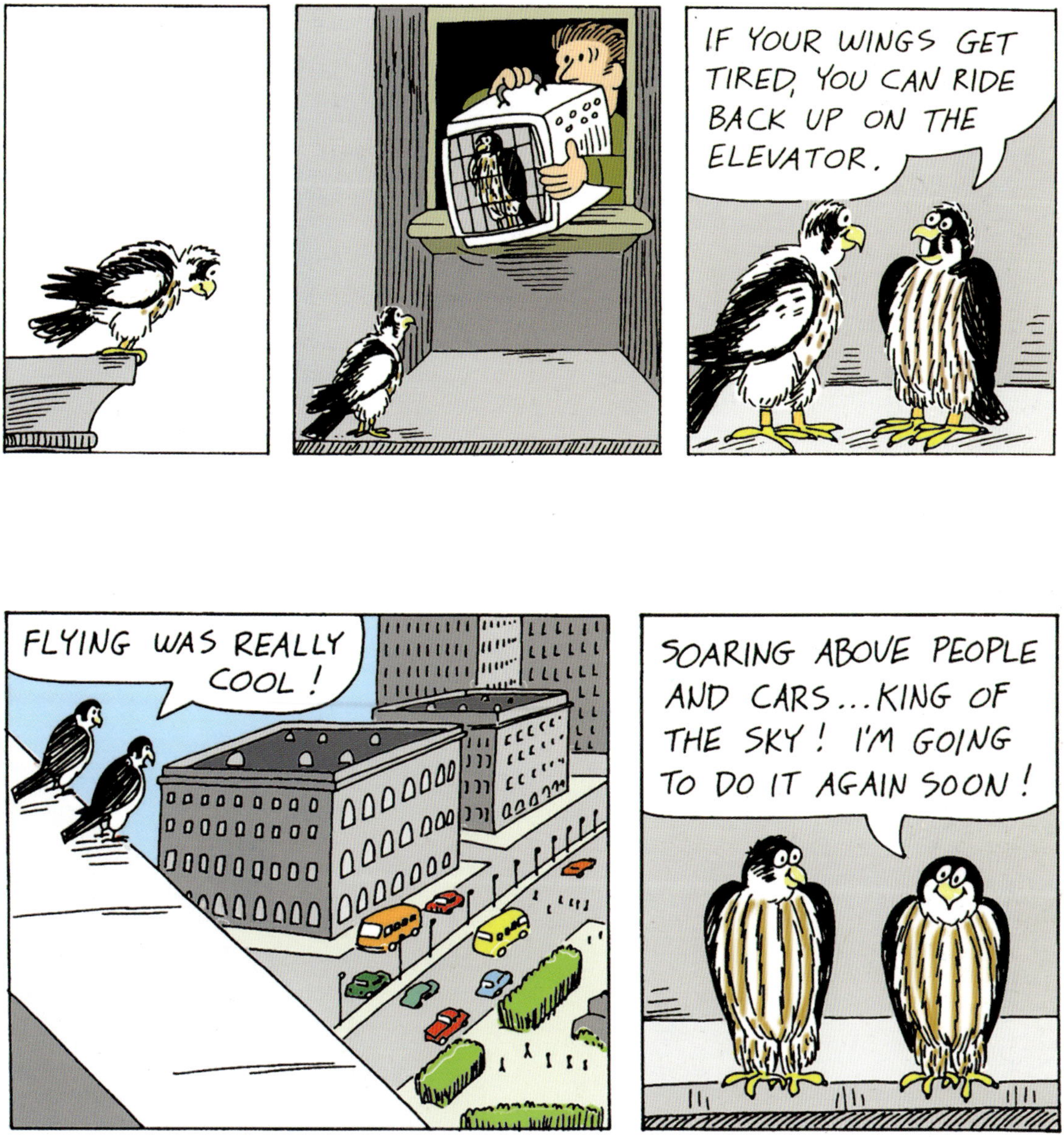
IF YOUR WINGS GET TIRED, YOU CAN RIDE BACK UP ON THE ELEVATOR.
FLYING WAS REALLY COOL!
SOARING ABOVE PEOPLE AND CARS... KING OF THE SKY! I'M GOING TO DO IT AGAIN SOON!

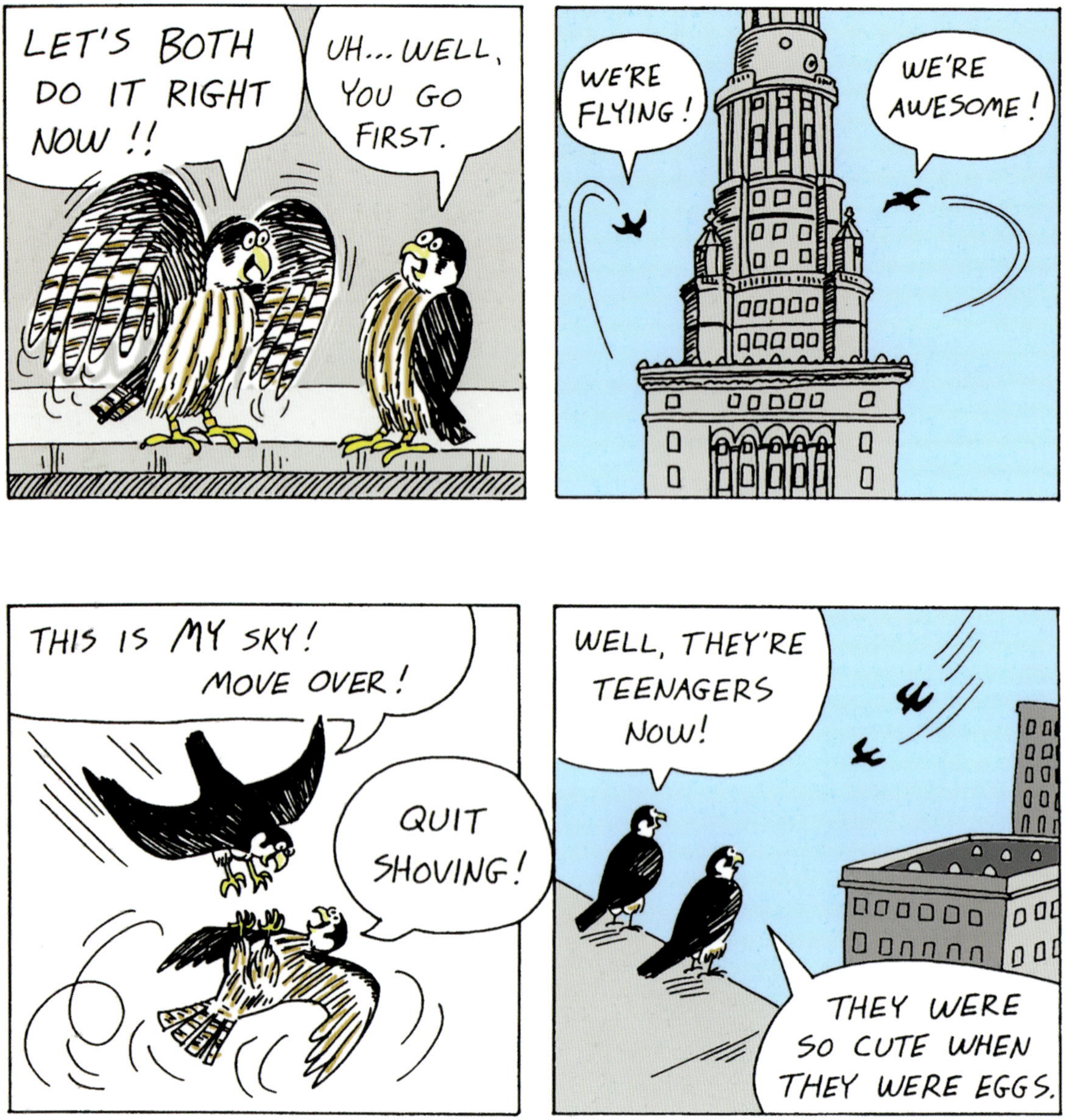
LET'S BOTH DO IT RIGHT NOW !!
UH... WELL, YOU GO FIRST.
WE'RE FLYING !
WE'RE AWESOME !
THIS IS MY SKY! MOVE OVER!
QUIT SHOVING!
WELL, THEY'RE TEENAGERS NOW!
THEY WERE SO CUTE WHEN THEY WERE EGGS.

Stars and Stripes flew away to live somewhere else. Since then falcons have nested on the same ledge. In many cities, falcons nest on tall buildings and often there are TV cameras watching them. There may be a falcon show where you live! To learn more, go to www.peregrinefund.org, www.birds-of-prey.org, and www.audubon.org.